301 209 .SUT

D1324678

Sut	Wat
WP	Co
Ch	Mc
RR	Rou S-S
Be	Mob

ROARY
The Racing Car

Stars 'N' Cars

LONDON BOROUGH OF SUTTON LIBRARY SERVICE (ROU)

30119 025 515 067	
Askews	Apr-2009
JF	

First published in Great Britain by HarperCollins Children's Books in 2008

10 9 8 7 6 5 4 3 2 1

ISBN-10: 0-00-727518-8   ISBN-13: 978-0-00-727518-2

© Chapman Entertainment Limited & David Jenkins 2008

A CIP catalogue record for this title is available from the British Library.
No part of this publication may be reproduced, stored in a retrieval system
or transmitted in any form or by any means, electronic, mechanical, photocopying,
recording or otherwise, without the prior permission of HarperCollins Publishers Ltd,
77-85 Fulham Palace Road, Hammersmith, London W6 8JB.
The HarperCollins website address is: www.harpercollinschildrensbooks.co.uk
All rights reserved

Based on the television series Roary the Racing Car and the original script
'Stars N Cars' by Dave Ingham.
© Chapman Entertainment Limited & David Jenkins 2008

Visit Roary at: www.roarytheracingcar.com

Printed and bound in China

Stars 'N' Cars

HarperCollins Children's Books

It was a fine morning at Silver Hatch racetrack. Big Chris had received a letter, and he was waving it around excitedly.

"What is it, Big Chris?" Marsha asked. "Yes, what is it?" repeated Roary and Cici. Maxi looked on, pretending not to be interested.

"Listen to this!" Big Chris yelled.

"I – that is ME – have been picked to compete on Karaoke TV!" Big Chris was so excited.

"What – the one on the telly?" Marsha asked.

"Yes! It's a dream come true – a dream come true!" babbled Big Chris.

A little while later, Big Chris was tuning Roary's engine and mumbling to himself. "I can't believe it. Karaoke TV. Me! What should I sing? Should I do a ballad or a fast one? I don't know..."

"I didn't know you were so serious about your singing, Big Chris," Roary said.

"Oh, yes, Roary," Big Chris replied, "I've always wanted to be a singer. It's my dream. And as I've always said, son, you've got to follow your dream."

Mr Carburettor came running in, excitedly.

"Big Chrissy, Big Chrissy," he called. "I'm so happy to hear you will be on TV... It's a wonderful opportunity to promote Silver Hatch! So, in return, Hellie will take you to TV land!"

"Why so sad, Roary?" asked Cici as she entered the workshop later.

"It's Big Chris, Cici. If he sings on Karaoke TV… and wins… he'll be a star! And then he'll leave us!"

"He can't leave us," said Cici. "He loves it here – and we need him!"

Roary brightened up.

"That's true! Maybe if we show him how much we need him, he'll stay! I've had an idea. Race you!" And off they both went. Suddenly, Roary slammed on his brakes.

Roary screeched off the track,
and straight into a muddy pool,
splashing Flash and his breakfast
carrot with mud. Cici just managed
to stop in time.

"Roary," she asked. "Are you
all right?"

"Yes," whispered Roary to Cici.
"It worked. Now you go and get
Big Chris to get me out."

"Oh, I see," said Cici. "Right!"
And she drove off to fetch
Big Chris.

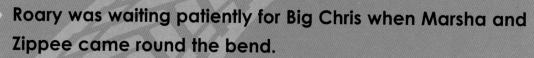

Roary was waiting patiently for Big Chris when Marsha and Zippee came round the bend.

"Oh, Roary. How did you end up there?" she asked.

"I took the bend too quickly, Marsha," replied Roary, "I skidded. But it's OK; Cici's gone to get Big Chris."

Just then Cici came back.

"Come on, Cici," said Marsha, "I'm sure between you and Zippee we can pull Roary out. Let's go."

And she hitched Zippee to Cici's bumper and by the time Big Chris arrived they had pulled him out.

"Oh good," said Big Chris. "You're out already. Well, at least you know you'll be in good hands when I'm gone, Roary." Roary's plan had failed!

Later, Roary was driving past a sleeping Rusty when he spotted Big Chris's karaoke costume on the washing line.

"If I hide Big Chris's costume, maybe he won't go on TV," Roary thought to himself. Quick as a flash, he pulled it off the line and took it to the workshop. When Big Chris saw that his suit had gone, he was amazed.

Then he panicked and went running into the workshop, shouting, "Has anybody seen my suit? Has anybody seen my suit?"

Roary was reading a magazine, pretending he'd been there all the time. But he hadn't had time to hide the suit properly.

A bit of it was sticking out of the oil drum he'd put it in.
Suddenly, Big Chris spotted it.

"Oh," he said. "Thank goodness for that. I'm so excited,
I must have put it there by accident!"

Roary had one last idea. To show Big Chris how much the cars appreciated him, he got all the cars together for a big parade just before Big Chris left. Big Chris was grateful, but he had to leave before the parade ended.

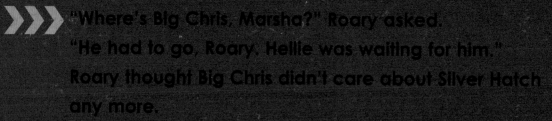 "Where's Big Chris, Marsha?" Roary asked.
"He had to go, Roary. Hellie was waiting for him."
Roary thought Big Chris didn't care about Silver Hatch
any more.
"Bye, Big Chris," he said sadly to himself.
"I hope you come back..."

When Big Chris was on TV, all the cars watched. He really went for it, and his singing was better than ever before. At the end of the song, he could hardly believe his ears when the presenter came over with a trophy.

"I think we've found our winner, ladies and gentlemen!" he said.

All the cars cheered for Big Chris. Only Roary was sad. Now he'd never see him again...

So he couldn't believe his eyes the next morning, when who should come into the workshop but Big Chris!
"Am I pleased to see you, Big Chris," Roary said, smiling.
"Oh, same here, Roary," said Big Chris, happily. "One day away from here is enough for me!"

"But what about following your dream?" asked Roary. "Well, I did," Big Chris replied, "I sang on Karaoke TV, and I even won! You see, singing may be my passion, but here with all my friends at Silver Hatch – well, that's where I belong."

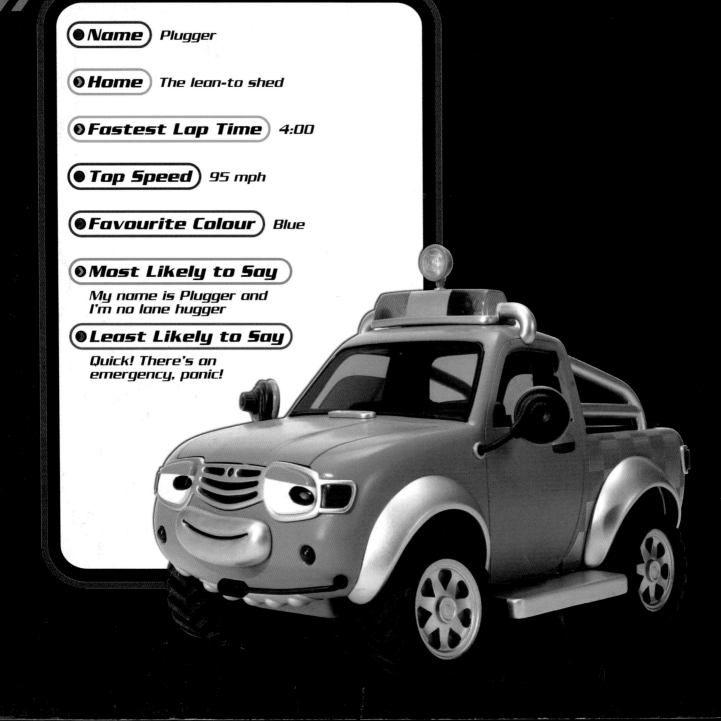

Name Plugger

Home The lean-to shed

Fastest Lap Time 4:00

Top Speed 95 mph

Favourite Colour Blue

Most Likely to Say

My name is Plugger and
I'm no lane hugger

Least Likely to Say

Quick! There's an
emergency, panic!

Plugger

Race to the finish line with these fun story and activity books.

Big Chris's Big Workout
Can Big Chris beat Marsha round the track?

Flash Flips Out
Roary's racing pal Flash in trouble!

Roary's First Day
Can Roary make a splash at Silver Hatch?

Pole Position Poster Book
Customise the cars with Roary!
48

Big Chris's Race Day Sticker Book
Help Big Chris get Roary ready to race!
40

Start your engines with Talking Big Chris!

Roary the Racing Car is out soon on DVD!

Rev up R/C Roary to race to victory!

Go Roary, go-oooo!

Get ready to race!

Light 'em up Roary!

As seen on TV milkshake! As seen on

Visit Roary at www.roarytheracingcar.com